Librarians

by Judith Jango-Cohen

Lerner Publications Company • Minneapolis

Dedicated to Burlington's librarians, a town treasure.
A big thanks to Gretchen Bierbaum, editor, and to Burlington
librarians Maria DelCheccolo, Helen Downes, Marie Gordinier,
Hermayne Gordon, Steve Levin, Rose Magliozzi, Charl Maynard,
Martha Ogren, Art Pinsoneault, and Lee Sylvester for
enthusiastically sharing their time and insights.

Text copyright © 2005 by Judith Jango-Cohen

Lerner Publications Company
A division of Lerner Publishing Group
241 First Avenue North
Minneapolis, MN 55401 U.S.A.

Website address: www.lernerbooks.com

Words in **bold type** are explained in a glossary on page 31.

Library of Congress Cataloging-in-Publication Data

Jango-Cohen, Judith.
    Librarians / by Judith Jango-Cohen.
      p. cm. – (Pull ahead books)
    Includes index.
    ISBN: 0-8225-1691-8 (lib. bdg. : alk. paper)
    1. Librarians—Juvenile literature. 2. Library science—
Vocational guidance—Juvenile literature. 3. Libraries—
Juvenile literature [1. Librarians. 2. Occupations.] I. Title.
II. Series.
Z682.J36 2005
020'.92–dc22   2003026051

Manufactured in the United States of America
1 2 3 4 5 6 – JR – 10 09 08 07 06 05

Are you looking for a great book?

Ask a librarian.

Librarians work in the library in your
community. Your community is made
up of people in your neighborhood, town,
or city.

Some librarians work in **public libraries.**
Others work in school libraries and
help students and teachers.

All librarians have gone to **college**. College is where people study after high school. Librarians study there for five or more years.

Librarians have lots to do. They buy books, magazines, newspapers, movies, and CDs for the library.

Librarians take care of library books.
They fix ripped pages. They protect
book covers with plastic. The plastic
helps the books last longer.

Librarians also keep track of everything in the library. How do they know where to find the books you need?

Librarians give each book a **label.**
Some labels have numbers. Animal
books have a "500" number.

500-599
SCIENCE
Astronomy
Rocks and Minerals
Plants
Animals

Labels also have letters. The letters might be part of the writer's name. Dr. Seuss wrote this book. His books are on the S shelf.

MEMORIAL LIBRARY MEDIA CENTER

30005104520   782.1 MON

Cinderella

Librarians also give each book a number called a **bar code.**

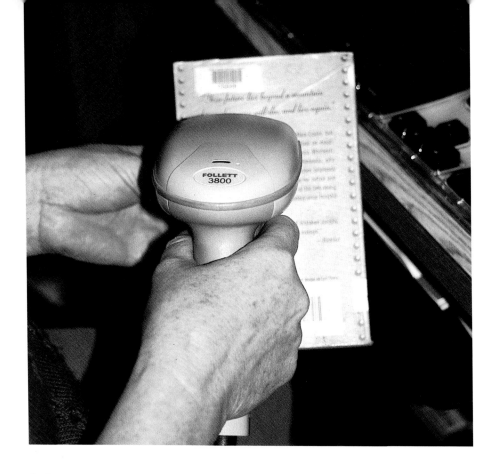

Librarians use the bar code. When you want to take a book home, they put the bar code on a list.

The list is on a computer. It helps librarians keep track of books people take home.

People return
piles of books
every day.
Librarians put
them all away.
But that's not
all a librarian
does.

Librarians also help people find **information.** Information is facts and ideas. It can be found in books, movies, magazines, and newspapers.

A library's globes and maps give
information too.

Librarians help people find information using computers.

What else do librarians do? They make cozy areas where people can read.

Librarians also set up quiet work spaces.

Sometimes librarians give programs.
Programs make reading extra fun.

Programs may be puppet shows, story hours, or sing-alongs.

Librarians hold book fairs. Readers
can buy new books at the book fair.

Librarians know how important books are.
Books help you learn. They make you
laugh. They make you think.

Librarians enjoy reading books. They
like new stories and old favorites too.

They enjoy books most when they
share them with you.

Facts about Librarians

- In America in the 1700s, only men were librarians. They kept track of books, dusted the shelves, and opened the library at least once a week.

- America's first woman librarian worked in Boston, Massachusetts, in 1856.

- A librarian named Melvil Dewey formed the American Library Association (ALA) in 1876. Every year, the ALA gives the Newbery and Caldecott awards to excellent children's books.

- Librarians work in more than 117,000 libraries throughout the United States.

- Some librarians know one subject very well. They work at special libraries for law, medicine, art, science, or music.

- Librarians at the Library of Congress take care of the largest library in the world. It has about 530 miles of bookshelves.

Librarians through History

- The first librarians lived 4,000 years ago in a country that is now called Iraq. These librarians took care of clay tablets, an early form of books.

- Librarians once copied words and pictures in books by hand. Hand-copied books were so precious that librarians chained them to heavy tables.

- America's oldest library is Rhode Island's Redwood Library. Librarians have worked there since 1750.

- In 1876, Melvil Dewey invented a way to organize books into one of ten groups. Art books get a "700" label. History books have a "900" label.

- In the early 1900s, librarians began bringing books to people in vans called bookmobiles.

More about Librarians

Books

Flanagan, Alice K. *Ms. Davison, Our Librarian.* New York: Children's Press, 1996.

Gibbons, Gail. *Check It Out! The Book about Libraries.* New York: Harcourt Brace Jovanovich, 1985.

Jaspersohn, William. *My Hometown Library.* Boston: Houghton Mifflin, 1994.

Simon, Charnan. *Librarians.* Chanhassen, MN: The Child's World, 2003.

Websites

American Library Association: Libraries & You
http:// www.ala.org/Template.cfm?Section=librariesandyou

"Do We" Really Know Dewey?
http:// www.Columbia.K12.mo.us/dre/dewey/

KidsClick! Web Search for Kids by Librarians
http:// www.kidsclick.org

What Does a Librarian Do?
http:// www.whatdotheydo.com/libraria.htm

Glossary

bar code: a long number on a library book. The bar code helps librarians keep track of the book.

college: a school where people study after they finish high school

community: a group of people who live in the same city, town, or neighborhood. Communities share the same fire departments, schools, libraries, and other helpful places.

computer: a machine used to store and find information

information: facts and ideas

label: a tag on a book that helps you find it on the shelf

public libraries: town or city libraries open to all people

Index

Photo Acknowledgments

The photographs in this book appear courtesy of: © Judith Jango-Cohen, front cover, pp. 4, 6, 9, 12, 13, 15, 16, 17, 18, 20, 22, 23, 24, 26, 27; © Cynthia Zemlicka/Independent Picture Service, pp. 3, 10, 19; © Eliot Cohen, p. 5; © John Henley/CORBIS, p. 7; © Nana Twumasi/Independent Picture Service, p. 8; © Todd Strand/ Independent Picture Service, pp. 11, 21; © Erin Liddell/Independent Picture Service, p. 14; © Stone Royalty Free by Getty Images, p. 25; © CORBIS, p. 29.